LISTENING TO MY FEELINGS

by Michael Gordon

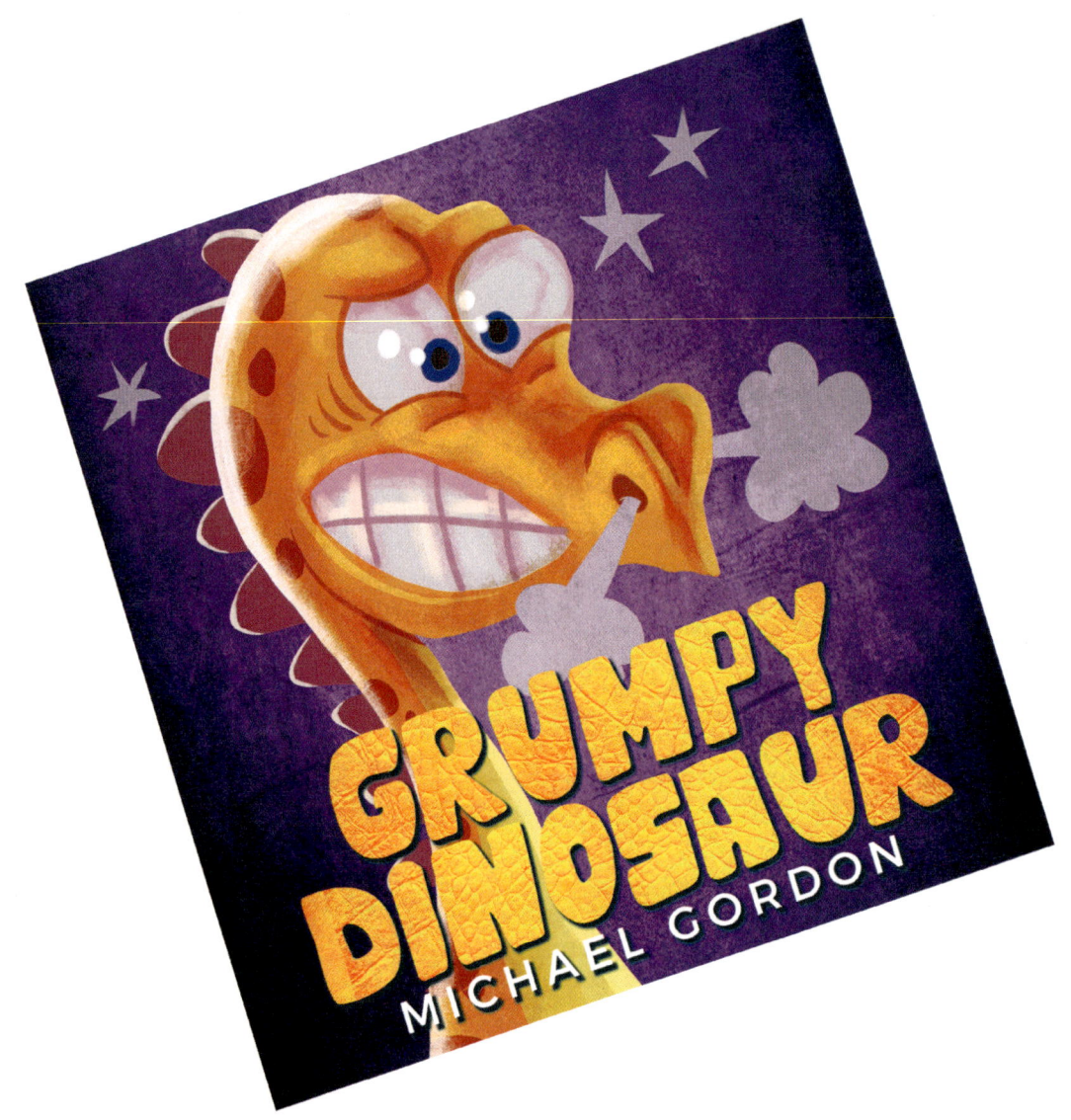

Go https://michaelgordonclub.wixsite.com/books **to get** "The Grumpy Dinosaur" for **FREE!**

THIS BOOK BELONGS TO

....

....

AGE: ....

Josh was was usually a well-behaved boy,
But sometimes he struggled with sharing his toys.
He loved his big sister and enjoyed when they'd play,
Until she picked up one of his toys one day.

That's when Josh's frustration would start to show.
He'd shout at his sister until she let go.

If she didn't put down his toy you would see
A boy as upset as a small boy can be.

Sister Emma took one of Josh's toys one day;

He got angry and shouted, then pushed her away.

He hit his sister and tried to push her once more.

Emma cried out loud and Mom rushed in through the door.

She saw Emma crying and feeling quite sad.
Mom looked sternly at Josh, but she didn't get mad.
She gave Emma a hug and told Josh to go.
Josh left looking sorry with his head hanging low.

When Mom asked, "What happened?" Josh's frustration showed. "When Emma took my toy, I felt like I'd explode."

"Feeling your feelings is always okay," Mom said.

"But you need to stay calm, so you don't lose your head."

"Hitting is never the right thing to do.
You love your sister and she loves you too."
Josh asked, "What can I do when I'm not feeling good?
I want to feel happy and behave like I should."

Mom and Dad talked to Josh about what happened that day
They told him how to make his bad feelings go away.

"Inhale like you're smelling sweet flowers," Mom said, "and then Exhale like you're blowing out candles. Then do it again."

"You must manage your feelings and not hit others," Dad said.
"Dancing, singing and hugs can help you feel good instead.
Do everything you can to get yourself feeling good
And if those things don't work then here's something that could."

"Imagine bad feelings are a ball and squeeze that ball tight. Then throw it far away with all of your might."

"I'll try doing those things," Josh said and hugged Mom and Dad. "I won't hit Emma again. I don't like feeling mad!"

That week, while shopping with Mom, Josh wanted something new.
When Mom said "no" he felt angry but knew what to do.
He breathed deeply, hugged Mom, and kept control of his head.
"You used your tools well, Josh, I'm so proud of you," Mom said.

Your opinion could change the word!

I hope you enjoyed this little story. Reviews from awesome customers like you help other parents to feel confident about choosing this book too.

Would you mind taking a minute to leave your feedback?

I will be forever grateful!

                Michael

About author

Michael Gordon is the talented author of several highly rated children's books including the popular Sleep Tight, Little Monster, and the Animal Bedtime.

He collaborates with the renowned Kids Book Book that creates picture books for all of ages to enjoy. Michael's goal is to create books that are engaging, funny, and inspirational for children of all ages and their parents.

Contact

For all other questions about books or author, please e-mail michaelgordonclub@gmail.com.

Award-winning books

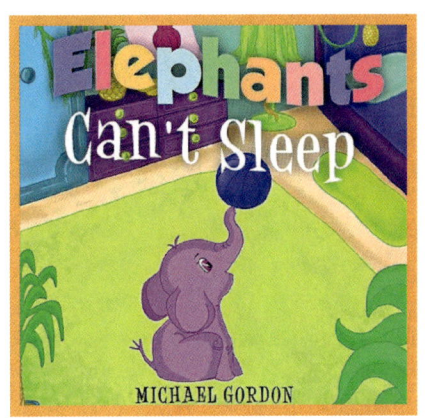

Elephants Can not Sleep

The

Little Elephant likes to break the rules. He never cleans his room. He never listens to mama's bedtime stories and goes to bed really late. But what if he tried to follow the routine so that the bedtime would become an amazing experience?

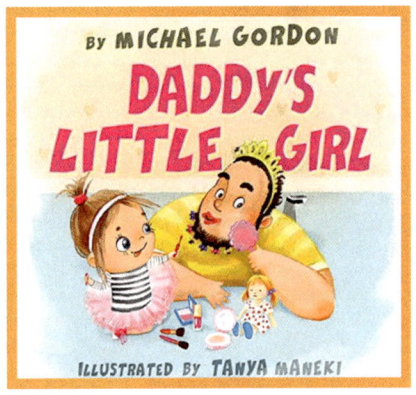

Little Girl's Daddy

the Who Needs a super hero the when you have your dad? Written in beautiful rhyme this is an excellent story that honors all fathers in the world.

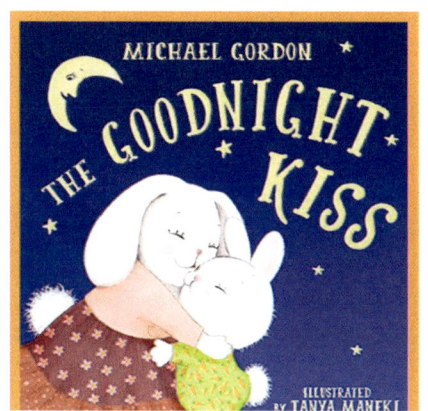

The Goodnight Kiss

Welcome to a cozy, sweet little bunny family. Mom is putting her little son Ben to bed, but she's not quite successful. Little boy still wants to play games and stay up late. Ben also likes to keep his mommy in his room at bedtime. Mrs. Bunny tries milk, warm blankets, books , and finally a kiss ... what will work?

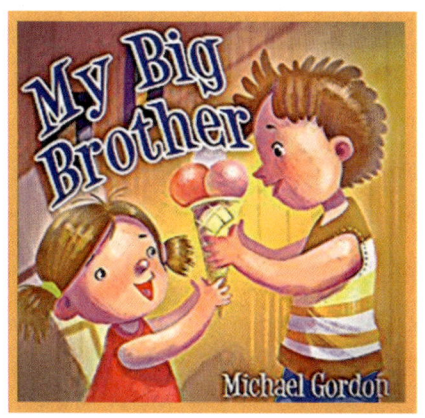

My Big Brother

The

Each of our lives will always be a special part of the other. There's Nothing Quite Like A Sibling Bond Written in beautiful rhyme this is an excellent story that values patience, acceptance and bond between a brother and his sister.

© 2019 Michael Gordon. All rights reserved.

All rights reserved. This book or parts thereof may not be reproduced in any form, stored in any retrieval system, or transmitted in any form by any means—electronic, mechanical, photocopy, recording, or otherwise—without prior written permission of the publisher, except as provided by United States of America copyright law.

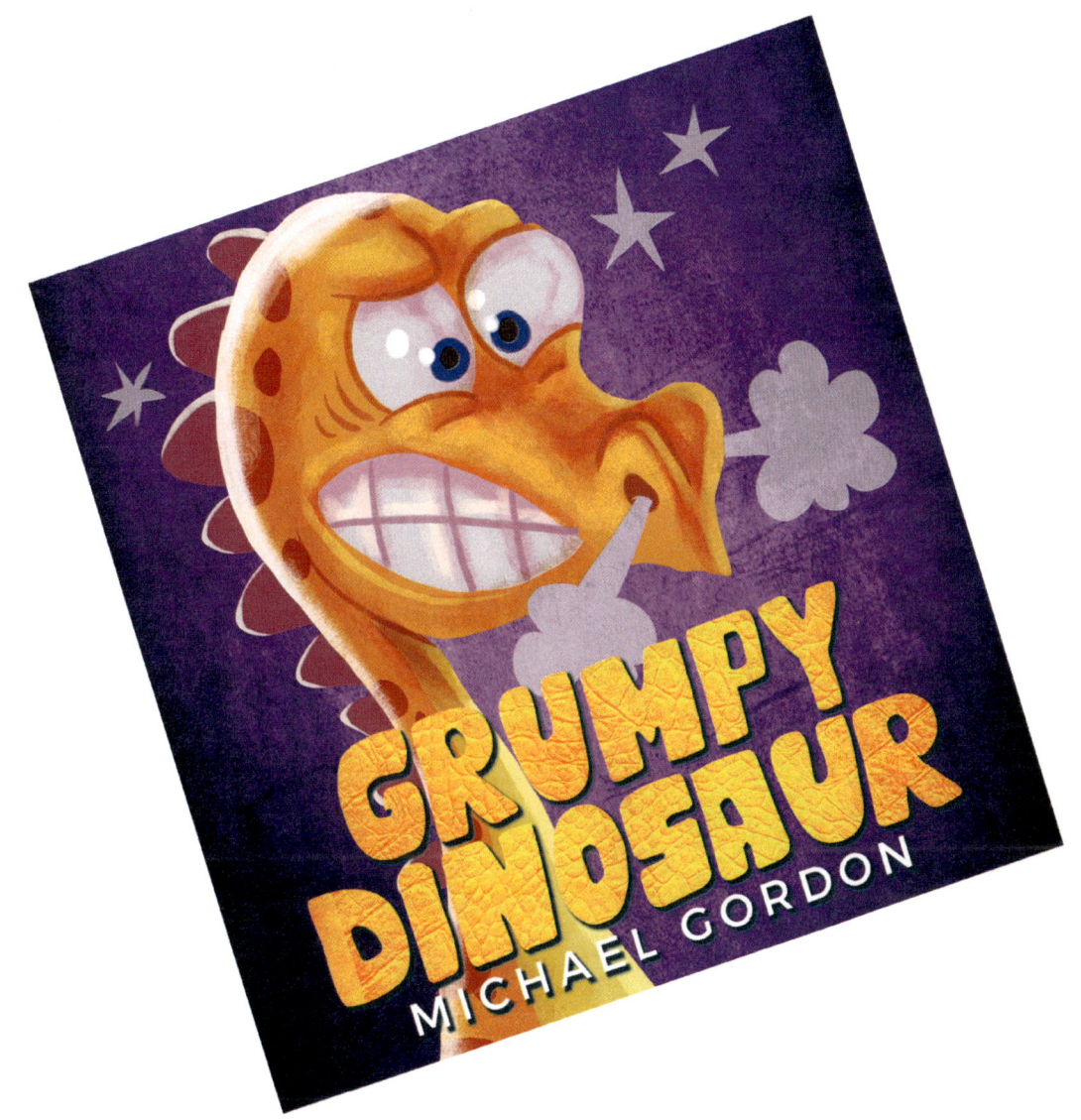

Go https://michaelgordonclub.wixsite.com/books **to get** "The Grumpy Dinosaur" for **FREE!**

Made in the USA
Columbia, SC
14 December 2020